DISCARD
D0786400

The UPROAR

The UPROAR

by Doris Orgel

pictures by Anita Lobel

McGRAW-HILL BOOK COMPANY
New York Toronto St. Louis San Francisco

 Library of Congress Catalog Card Number: 72-111992 1234567890 HDEC 7876543210

Saul Laurence's mother had a soft, wispy
dress on, the color of moonlight and stars out.
"Where are you going?" Saul Laurence asked.

She lifted him up and held him high over her head.
"To Madame Butterfly," she said.
"Who is that?" asked Saul Laurence.
"A lady in an opera," his mother explained.
"In an uproar?" asked Saul Laurence
His mother gave a little laugh, ting-a-ling, like
the triangle Saul Laurence played at play school.

Saul Laurence didn't laugh. He was thinking about
Madame Butterfly and about the uproar. And he wondered
why his parents wanted to go. . . . Because at home they were
almost always quiet, they hardly made any noises.

"I wish *I* could go," Saul Laurence said.
His mother smiled. She swung him down from over
her head, and landed him — plonk — on his bed.

His father came in. "We'd better hurry," he said,
"because the opera house is far away."
Saul Laurence took his father by the necktie, a
long one with big stripes across. And he said,
"*I* want to go to the uproar house. Take *me*."
His father laughed, "Ho, ho," loud and deep, and
told him, "You'd better go to sleep. Mrs. Onion is here."
Saul Laurence dived under his blanket.
"Good night, son," his father said.
"Good night," said his mother. And she kissed him
on the blanket where she thought his nose might be.

Mrs. Onion's name was really something else. But she usually wore a sweater over her dress, and a coat over the sweater, and a raincoat over the coat in case of rain. And before she sat down she peeled the raincoat off the coat, the coat off the sweater, and the sweater off the dress —

just like, one time when no one was watching,
Saul Laurence had peeled the skin off the skin
off the skin off the skin off an onion,
until only a little bit of an onion was left.
All the while, smelling the onion had made tears
in his eyes. Seeing Mrs. Onion could do that, too.

Saul Laurence did not like her.
And he hated the way she sang to him,

"N o w I l a y m e d o w n t o s l e e p"

all wobblingly, and wrong.

Pretty soon Mrs. Onion came into his room. She peeked under his blanket. Saul Laurence kept his eyes shut, tight, tight. Mrs. Onion thought he was sleeping. She did not sing — and that was lucky, because the noise of "Now I lay me" would certainly have kept Madame Butterfly away.

Mrs. Onion went out and shut the door.

In came Madame Butterfly, through the window.
She was the color of moonlight,
and her wide wings shimmered in the dark.

"Come with me," she said.
She took Saul Laurence by the hand,
and flew with him into the night.

Above them were stars. Beside them were clouds. Smoke stacks and television antennas pointed up from below. Still farther below them, way, way down, buses, trucks, and taxicabs went by, no bigger than the buses, trucks and taxis Saul Laurence sometimes raced across his bureau top.

They flew and they flew, over avenues and streets,
over a park, over a fountain splashing frothy water up,
and through a tall, tall window into the uproar house.

Inside it were more men and ladies than Saul Laurence had ever seen, sitting all around. And in the middle was a stage, for Madame Butterfly and him.
Everyone looked up at them and waited. . . .

Madame Butterfly smiled,
and with the softest, wispiest
noise in the world,
she folded her wings, Whhrr, whhsh!
That was the start of the uproar.
Everyone applauded.

Then a short, gray-haired lady
not far from the stage stood up.

She put her head forward.
She closed her eyes and opened her mouth.
She quacked, once, twice, again, three such calm
and perfect quacks, no duck could have uttered them better.
Everyone applauded.

Next, farther back, a man with a moustache stood up. He balled his fists and gave a low, lumbering, rumbling, louder, louder, crackling, crashing summer evening thunderbolt. Some people trembled at it. Others applauded. Saul Laurence, by Madame Butterfly's side, trembled *and* applauded.

More and more people stood up.
Soon all the ladies and men in the uproar house were standing up,
making noises, all together.

Saul Laurence listened very hard. He heard:

Soda fizz. A train arrive. A typewriter, clickety, quick.
Cymbals. A neigh. Splosh, a dive. A tennis ball, thwok, thwok.
An oboe, Yes, yes. Wuff, wuff. A book page turn.
A telephone. Elephants stampeding. Sigh.
A propeller whirr. A footstep.
Plop, an egg. A door open. Gurgle. A breeze. A torrent.

He heard noises so tiny that in any other place not even mice might have heard them.
He heard noises so enormous they would have blown the roof off any other house.

He heard noises by the thousands,
all the men's and ladies' favorite noises in the world,
each noise exactly right, and not one "Now I lay me" among
them — oh, what a wonderful uproar!

Suddenly he heard a hush.
It was a greater hush than he had ever heard.
And the men and ladies all around were looking up at him.
Lightly, lightly, Madame Butterfly touched him on the lips.
That meant, it's *your* turn now! So, in the silence,
Saul Laurence made the noise of a snowflake falling.

Then, a chirp-a-chirp. Then more of his favorite noises,
one after the other, each exactly right:
A new miaow. Carrunch. Cuckoo. A merman sing. Rustle.
Whistle. Zoom. Plck, plck, gallipity, gallopoty,
bzzzzz, brrrrrrm, rrrrroooo OOAR!

Everyone applauded him, and shouted, "More, more, MORE!"

So then Saul Laurence tried to make the noise of the triangle
he played at play school — and just at that moment
he heard it quite distinctly, ting-a-ling, ting-a-ling.
It came from quite far away, and right near by. . . .

Saul Laurence still heard it, flying back through the night
with Madame Butterfly. . . .

Then he opened his eyes that had been shut tight, tight,
and thought with a pang he might see Mrs. Onion peeking
at him, and hear her sing to him all wobblingly, and wrong.

But no, instead he still heard ting-a-ling, and saw his mother.
She kissed him on the nose.
"It was a wonderful opera," she said.

The Author

The mother of three lively children, DORIS ORGEL knows the full meaning of the word, "uproar." She is the author of many distinguished books for children, including the recent novel, **Next Door to Xanadu, In a Forgotten Place,** and the popular **Sarah's Room. The Uproar** represents her first collaboration with Anita Lobel.

The Artist

ANITA LOBEL received her art training in Sweden and the United States. An author-artist in her own right, Mrs. Lobel has won widespread recognition for such books as **The Troll Music, Sven's Bridge,** and **Potatoes, Potatoes.** She lives in Brooklyn with her artist husband Arnold Lobel, and their two children.